THE STORM AND THE STRIFE

PALMETTO
PUBLISHING
Charleston, SC
www.PalmettoPublishing.com

The Storm and the Strife
Copyright © 2023 by Gabbiano Gatto

All rights reserved

Hardcover ISBN: 979-8-8229-2828-2
Paperback ISBN: 979-8-8229-2745-2
eBook ISBN: 979-8-8229-2746-9

THE STORM AND THE STRIFE

GABBIANO GATTO

1

There have always been lovers in controversy, and though their affairs may have lasted beyond the burdens of their separation, this one was doomed from the start.

Albrecht had been in his music room for years before Sofia moved into his building. He had always had the far corner of the hall. He had always dressed very casually. He was sometimes very intense and never at times very talkative, and all the time very lazy, though he sometimes roused himself from sleep shortly after midnight. He was in every way withdrawn from the world and its confrontations. He excelled in Brahms, expressed himself in Chopin, and harbored the spirit of Rachmaninoff. He was abrupt, he was fluent and he had older more experienced interpretation of the music which he played. At this time in his life, however, he was dressed up with nowhere to go. He made his recordings with promises from the local academy, but still there was no one. No one to defend him or attend to him. He came and went back and forth to the academy only on days when it was not a chore. The rest of his time was spent at home in quiet interpretation of piano by the window down the hall where very few people could hear him. He had two pianos, a Fabbrini and a D'Almaine. He played only the Fabbrini at home, using the D'Almaine at the academy where it was kept only for him. When he approached his piano, it was with an affinity for original interpretation, but all the time it was like push and pull at the keys, representing an impulse he had, like one that laid down the music with adulteration. In effect, he was sexy, and his hands and his fingers were outspoken. Emphatically so the left, where the withdrawal from touching the ivory is slow, and there it is nubile and it is born somehow royal, somewhat majestic at times. The right hand was dominant, but like the act of self-gratification, he was without any kind of passionate intensity for repetition in movement or phrase. Instead, he rebounded through those staves with a bias for the variations that he loved. When a piece was somewhat unconventional, his interpretive became somehow exotic, and his ascending and descending scales bordered on tickling, such as of a child or a lover. Observations made by his audiences included the view that his playing was like a representation of earthly life with its conquests and defeats, rises and falls, and when represented by his playing, seems ceaseless and undying.

2

Then there was Sofia, the young woman who lived down the hall, at its opposite end. In her music room was a piano, a viol, a cello and two violins, one of which was an original Stradivarius. There was one leather couch in the living room. It was black and cold and it evoked icicles on the back of her legs, so she let it sit unused.

She brought take-out to her kitchenette on a fine Thursday afternoon after a sleepless night. She had not fixed a meal earlier in the day because she had been too tired to cook. Now she felt like one who had never eaten before.

She didn't have a television and she had never bought a set of silverware or glasses, but had only taken what was given to her by others. She had copious amounts of belongings, such as articles of clothing, furniture, bedspreads, and shoes which were never worn. She collected the papers and programs of performances and art exhibits as often as she collected advertisements for the discreet services of other women. They were piling up in boxes and on shelves and in the corner of the music room.

After leaving her takeout on the counter, she turned to face her music once again, developing an hatred for her moments of jealousy of other women, because she considered her life without a baby. She thought of her inexhaustible energy and what it was doing to her body and her mind. She let the thought pass without judgment for that energy and that jealousy were her clay to mold and to form.

Albrecht splashed on some *di Gio*, then he extrapolated the elements of a newspaper in print. The academy called during his reading of the collectible books markets, so he saved his place and answered the phone. He divested himself of his complaints to the director, and when he had hung up, he went to his kitchen and he washed, and then strained and prepared bunches of red seedless grapes. He spooned out peach yogurt into a stainless steel bowl and then combined them and ate.

In his apartment he ruled and he ordered. There on a ledge were his watches and timepieces. There on his couch were the blankets and the throws of the past, protecting it from dust and stain. There was dust and there was lint. The carpet was a shade of maroon, and the lamp covers were still wrapped in plastic. The mangoes and the avocados were ripening on the tabletop. On his walls hung paintings and nude figure drawings of a famous historical muse, apparently one never to have been a life model.

Sofia's bills were paid. Her apartment was warm. She was thankful but ungratified and as she finished her rehearsal, she entered her bathroom to put on her blush. First she plucked and tweezed, and she exfoliated and epilated her body from head to toe, as well as her pubic hair. She dried off at the mirror paying attention to every redoubt and recoil of her sculpted physique. It had been cool and comfortable in the cascading water before she eventually made the application of makeup to her face in the mirror. Her impression of herself was better than what other people were saying about her, and that gave her the self-confidence she needed to pursue any man she was potentially interested in.

Sighing, she walked nude through the kitchen and into the hall where she lit incense, after which she threw on a kimono and ate her takeout with porce-lain chopsticks.

Albrecht's apartment was not just another place to exhibit his picture frames. He stacked his shelves with folded clothes in grays and browns and in black, because there was just much too much color in the world. He was tired of the squish-squish of the carpet and of the confinement, and he was angry about the cawing of the crows. The featurelessness of the furniture, the void of personality and the lack of a woman or two to make sense of the self, were all too much to bear.

As Sofia finished her meal she roamed her flat and wondered about a song. A love song between two mythical, mystical creatures carrying on through space or through the ocean, like there was between whales. What would it sound like? What would it sound like to a man? What would it look like if it could be seen? Would it be blues and browns? Would it have a face or would it have two? Would it be gorgeous? Would it be rigid? Should it sound conversational or commanding, or would it sound like *Moonlight*, the most hated of all sonatas, in her opinion. She thought it would have a furious pace: quick and fast, with a bassoon and a piccolo and a supporting character of strings.

Albrecht loved to read and was a purveyor of fine expensive books in every edition. Some were gold bound, some with rough edges and some in leather binding. Others were new and many were from fine collections that he'd had money to pay for. That Thursday he walked the sidewalk to the bookstore to shop for additional books for his own collection.

While at home, Sofia played the Kreisler's *Praeludium* in allegro in preparation for her appearance at the Metropolitan, when suddenly she changed her performance to Sarasate's *Habanera*.

Having concluded his purchase, Albrecht stomped out of the bookshop, very singular in mind as he very carefully avoided the faces of the avenue thereon, and he searched for a song in his head....

. . . when Sofia suddenly interrupted her passage of *Habanera* after a minute or two in avoidance of the false conclusion that the piece elicited in her mind, and turned instead to create something soft and sweet and confessing.

As Albrecht continued to approach his apartment, he felt himself on the edge of a path into social distortion and came nearer to a conclusion about his solitary hobby as book collector. But he was in no position to take up anything else, so when he arrived back home he turned his attention toward the care of an entire series of Arabic poetry in the hand of the poet, Imru al-Qais. He was not a native French speaker and his Hugo and his Voltaire were only half read; especially the Hugo, because *The Hunchback* was so deplorable in his opinion. What he preferred was the Italian in terms of romance, especially the Dell'Arte in treatise. In his art classes in college (because it had been an elective at that time) he would try to imitate the portraiture of Modigliani. His image of beauty had always rolled with the passing waves. He often saw the long faces and the almond shaped eyes, slightly crossed, as defensible, not only because they reminded him of his mother, but also because they appeared to him to have a graceful long neck, and he found that alluring.

After the recital and before her appearance, Sofia took the time to feed her pair of Siamese cats she kept because they were a gift from a man living in the islands. She had no time for recordings or for books or for *most* men after all, with the possible exception of one.

She lit a scented candle and she looked at old photos. Photos of men whom she thought represented the father she never had. At some point in the coming days, she would think of the old photos and when she sat and leafed through them again, she would be saddened and alone because her mother had passed away. So she stood in her bedroom with her violin and she personified from Gluck, a disparaging melody for the sake of self-pity because hers was so often a forgotten story.

3

The winter came and went and when Sofia recited with her violin she would play a song like the wailing of an approaching storm, a rainstorm of spring, and a song that reminded her of her own need to have a baby, and she felt defeated. But she had hope for one particular man.

His name was Albrecht. He had dark hair and dark brown eyes that projected a misery. She waited at the door to room 216. She had been awakened by a commotion in the hall early in the day. She had been satisfying her hunger earlier in the morning. It had been toast and oil for healthy, sensible living. Now she stood in the hallway and she stared. She stared at a man who was worth admiring. His sleeves were loose, his shirt was ruffled and his shoes were exposing black socks. He stood tall, relaxed and had no stubble. He was engaged in conversation with a neighbor briefly but did not look attentive. He spied her playfully, and they were on the verge of something momentarily, but it vanished. She wanted it back.

He invited her over to his apartment one weekday afternoon when she had been home from work. He was preoccupied yet very eagerly searching for someone, and she resisted the impulse to take him by the hand. He had gestured toward his room with one outstretched arm and an unsteady hand. He seemed to her to be very lazy. He put his hand into his pocket and trudged back toward his room. Her eyes had followed and then pleaded for affection from him with simply her presence at his door. She felt his depth serenely and his tortured nature all the more. When he merely sat and played piano, she pushed the door just slightly closed, and snuck away quickly, back to her room to prepare an avocado and sulk and empathize.

During the melancholy, she had to overcome small physical details, such as struggling with the appliances and negotiating the distance from the sink to the faucet or handling the weight of the pots and pans. Alone, she was challenged by no man or woman other than Albrecht. His room was a new and undiscovered land at the end of the hall.

She thought she heard the soft raindrops and the elements of a shower coming from his apartment. Something was making her wish he hadn't been so enticing, but she ached, and she couldn't leave well enough alone. She adjusted her jeans and she followed her instincts, going back to his room as if he were leading her. She peeked into his doorway. It was strewn from end to end with books. They looked unread, unopened and unused. He sat facing the piano toward a window which let in no light, like he and the music he played were expecting some great big moment, like a burst of sunlight, a breakthrough of success. Without taking her eyes off of him, she put herself on his couch, and she lay, head on the headrest, feet at the end crossing her one leg over the other and gazing toward the window with her arm over her forehead, entranced. She listened, but she was frantic in her anticipation of a physical connection, something he could manifest toward her with his arms and his hands and his posture-rocking her as he did- moving back and forth on the bench, never seeing her, never speaking, always interrupting her fantasies with another crescendo. But there was no bitter end yet. And as he left the piano and said good night she felt as though she were treading water helplessly but he had not offered her his hand.

4

He was fit and he was challenging but he had left her behind, struggling. From her point of view he was a distant apogee unable to be ascended. He was removed and he stayed away. It was a week later when she approached him again.

His door was open as usual.

He pounded and interrupted every semblance of music. He couldn't alliterate his phrases or elucidate his meaning. He was angered and it was disturbing.

He can't express how he feels toward me, she thought. He couldn't put it into his words or his music yet. He only stuttered and it was a musical salad of wrong notes, interrupted with banging as he hammered and pounded and pounded some more. She lay on the couch uncomfortably, unable to seep into the cushion, only struggling to endure. She was shaking slightly as she attempted to massage her forehead. When it was over, she was relieved yet unsettled. She trudged the usual hallway and path back to her apartment assuming that he was saying something she just didn't understand. *Concepts that eluded me*, she thought.

She surveilled his apartment from then on and got to know the wear and tear of his keep and the rise and fall of his patterns of living like where he stood to brush his teeth, all very much a mystery at first. She hoped to change him and turn him outside in, until he no longer cared about the carpet or the amount of time he ran the water or how many times he made coffee. So she removed the plastic from the lamp covers and replaced the batteries in the remotes and she cleaned up the nightmares in the laundry congregating in the corner of his room.

When back at her own place, Sofia commanded her next several pieces at her violin. While she hummed intermittently throughout each, she emphasized parts that would have been sung in his baritone voice.

They connected from time to time. She frequented his place, but *he* never visited *her*. Then he began pushing her away. He told her he was too busy. He had work to do, he claimed, or she was too eager or not his type. He tried soothing her with his apologies.

But she returned anyway.

He continued to resist her. This time it was with a cold shoulder and ignorance. Weeks went by. Sofia, alone, walked past the daily avenues outside of the Metropolitan. The simple pleasures were not amounting to anything anymore. The food tasted different and simply eating, itself, lacked meaning. It was not sustaining her life anymore. She needed his presence to go on. She would have settled for some kind of interlude. She struggled with daily chores. Cupboards slammed. Sun was blinding until she needed it dark in the room. Everything had weight. Unbearable and unfathomable weight. She stood to eat or she couldn't get through it at all.

Albrecht had risen up in a rebellion and had escaped from her laws of gravity. Day after day he was locked away in his ivory tower. *How can he resist me*, she thought. He was too strong. Too square. Too chaste. There was no contrition. *Why was he prolonging this?* She thought: *Was any of what she was hoping for, going to be possible?*

Then the situation changed and he began to take an interest in her again.

Once he became serious about her, and they began seeing each other steadily, she realized that she had been unprepared for the fame and the esteem that his age and his tenure at the academy brought into her life. She went with him to his black tie events and wore that slinky black dress, and she spun around like a girl unrestricted. She was hit on, and men made passes at her. She sold herself as a player, a master of that fine instrument, her violin. She learned all the right phrases and used all the right words, and made all the right glances, as though she had been born with enough social graces and fit to play the role of Albrecht's wife. He was indeed a very lucky man that day.

There was just one small inconvenience- she wasn't paid what she was worth. She made events and recitals and performed in chamber groups, but made very little ripple in the larger music world.

Her position made for a condition of anxiety and depression, so she sought medical treatment. Her doctor told her that she needed to take steps to remove stress from her life and she should engage in the art of mindfulness, for happiness and health and neuro-plasticity that could benefit her performance. So on Saturday she sat and watched the falling snow, and made a list of all the colors she saw, and the foods she ate and entered into Albrecht's room at the end of the hall where she observed and admired his scotch labels and his vase, bending at the waist and ogling the nooks and crannies of his sculptures.

5

When Albrecht went home one evening, it was dark, so he turned on one of five lamps, and wiped off walls and washed out sinks, and took the laundry to the washer. When he had finished watching a film concerned with the Munich chapter of the Social Democrat Movement during the time in between the world wars, he put on something more comfortable and he lifted a large volume of photographic nudes from the ledge next to his timepieces and he turned the massive pages, letting his eye work them while he hovered over the black and white images. Male and female. He marked the pages of his favorites: Female. Monochrome. A cutaway of the torso only, from knee to shoulder in contortion with shadow. All the while, the music in the background livened his activities.

Then he lost connection with the outside world again.

It was night. He reclined on his expensive futon with the navy sheets, the black comforter, and the gray pillow, because colors didn't belong in the room. For days when he could only remember the faces and the eyes of the people on the avenue, he used the green sheets and the black comforter while he wore the black shorts and a black tanktop in the bedroom. His black leather duffels in the closet were full of scarves and gloves and hats. One contained sexy lingerie for some woman on some other day if his luck was good. Then came Sofia one night, knocking the secret knock.

That night, she had come out of her virgin vault to perform for him in lacey panties, so he photographed her in black and white.

Waiting for each other was torture. There was a deficit in the amount of attention Sofia paid to the comforts she was used to making for herself. She placed herself in mock situations. Worrisome enactments of different scenarios. Skit after skit. Uncertain of which may be a real future for the two of them.

Albrecht shook. He paced. Unable to manage his emotions, he left the apartment, but she lingered there alone, while he walked the avenue to his post office, produced his key and opened his box and removed his magazines in brown paper, knowing that they were book catalogs and archaeology journals and gazettes. The trip did something for his nerves. Being down-town without the usual faces and the crowds, left him with feelings and sensations like tumbling down and away into the ash of a burning cigar, or thumbing the pages of a book as if to feel the slight rush of air escaping the edge of the pages. When he passed through the indoor shops and shuttled across the marble floor, it gave him a feeling of largesse that contained him from head to toe.

At his apartment, Sofia thought that Albrecht was all over with. In another sense she felt as though she were dangling over a cliff. It was no longer the featurelessnes, nor the measure of his commitment which angered her. It was Albrecht's departure from a melody. His divergence from a plot that made up her expectations of their story together, and how it should end. She wanted to draw away from it. It was the wrong orchestration. It was taking her nowhere, and out of the picture. His cadenzas no longer answered her vibrato. She looked away toward the door, toward home. It hurt her and he was hurting her. Maybe it was hurting *him* too.

6

The day was Saturday and Sofia listlessly trod the path forward down the usual hallway toward his door and found it open for the first time in a while. She walked in. Albrecht was there displaying his mastery at the piano once again. She was now in uncharted territory. She moved with effort, gazing at his figure for response. She had no idea what to do, so she picked up a book, and she retreated to the couch, not sure why she lacked the strength to tell him what as fair and what wasn't.

She lay in the usual position, and she approached the book from its back cover. On it was a foggy day in a green landscape with sloping hills.

She opened the book and read from the beginning.

"A man opened a door and walked into a room. He was a laborer in a mine and his clothes were stained and he smelled foul. He spoke to a man at a desk about a possible new vein deeper in the shaft, covered by water, but they quibble over details such as tools and lack of manpower. He leaves, unsettled. The man at his desk then folds up his writing paper and puts away his pen. He inserts the paper into an envelope and perches it at the corner of his desk. He rises from the desk and he goes to the hook. He peels off his overcoat from the hook and he slips into the figure of a businessman. He appropriates the letter and exits the room, bound for the town. His horse made a slow gallop as the road was muddy. He can see the town in the distance and he hurries on. The townsfolk there are busy. *And backward,* he thought. He proceeds down a path to the avenue of businesses and he makes a turn to a door marked for speculation.

Inside he produces his letter and argues over finance and the need for more men. A woman overhears them as she is hanging out there at the corner in need of work. She can no longer keep a roof over her head or fend for herself. Her bills gone unpaid and her mouth full of hunger, she is tired from lack of sleep. She needs this man. His business at an end, the man leaves the room, and there out in the air he finds the destitute young woman. He looked her up and down, repugnant at the onset, then admiring her for some reason, why, he wasn't sure, he couldn't put a finger on it. He beckoned her to him:

"I am in need of a housemaid," said the man.

"And I am in need of a job," replied the woman.

"Then you will be coming home with me today, if you can start right away. You will see what I need you to do."

On a horse, he lead her off into the countryside, headed back to the mine and its properties."

Sofia concluded the first chapters of the book, then placed it at the table near the couch. Albrecht's playing had ended and she galloped back to her apartment in awe of a mine.

7

The next day Sofia returned and she read from his book again, while Albrecht sat at his piano.

"At the expanse of the mine there is much moving about and there are men ready to begin new plans. He brings her to his property and she is led by her impulses and her hunger. They move on. At the door she observed him enter the room and remove his coat. At his request, she quickly passes from room to room taking note of her surroundings. There she will be working, there she will be fixing his meals, and there she would sleep. Moving back and forth in the house, he stops to say very little, and several times casually brushes up against her in the hall. There are armaments and maps that adorn his walls. She spent time in his kitchen where there was iron and fire and very much good food, but she is not yet tempted to eat, because he has not told her she can do so. At his request, she washed his clothes and set out his toiletries.

It grew dark and became night. The maid heard the man in the other room as she finished her chores. He was letting out grumbling and burly noises. She returned again to her chamber and to her meager establishment and she began undressing for bed. There is more noise. She pulls down the straps of her dress and pulls out her pins and she slips into bed. She is wishing to prepare for him a place where she can discover the mystery of that man.

She blew out the candle and drifted off to sleep."

As Sofia closed the book she realized the playing had stopped and she departed from the room again, wishing that she had not yet met the man who had settled in the room down the hall, because she felt that she wanted to play the role with him. She left the room and the door ajar and padded softly back to her bedroom.

There on his couch the next day, she opened the book to where she left off.

"It is day and the business of the mine is not yet over. The man is at the end of a shaft and his hands are filled with tools and his back is covered in rock and debris. From where he kneels, he pulls rocks from the wall exposing the vein. It is deep and wide and it is glittering like mad. He hacked and he piked and he burnished it smooth with his bare hand to take a look. He prayed to himself that it may not be another lode of worthless ore, but he sees it is indeed fine gold.

He took out a rock hammer and pried away bits for valuation. At the end of the day he bore back the bulk of his find, saying goodbye to the workers as he made toward the house where his maid had been kept from her chores by her thoughts. At the sight of him approaching, she went back to work. He lifted himself and his pack up the stairs and into the room pausing to take her in with his eyes, which settle on her. She blushed and noticed his dirt and his fatigue, and she wordlessly drew him a bath. He put down his pack for the valuing to be done later. In the bathroom he stood as she peered through the door without him knowing. He stood at the large basin on the floor and took off his shirt. He picked up the cloth and as he stood in the water he wrung out the water down his back. She watched as he ran his palm down his forearm and up onto his shoulder, then between it and his head, then up and down the back of his neck. She stayed hidden. She was gripping the frame of the door very unknowingly when he completely let go of his pants. She was pounding in her heart with fear to be seen appreciating his beauty and his chisels and his curves.

When it was over she retreated from the room and hurried down the hallway, all with him unaware.

The week continued and the man's wife returned from her place at the congress. She was as pasty and white as the white cliffs of Dover and she was up in arms all of the time. She pulled the weight of the household. The maid went unnoticed. She now had a rival. The maid felt as though her hopes had been crushed. The man and the maid could not share a moment, for they were constantly being embarrassed by the wife. His wife was not kind to the maid and showed no expressions of love for her husband either. The young maid watched the two of them in their dining room and she wished him to sneak a moment to be alone with her instead. The maid was angry. He saw her but he did not show that he recognized her in any way other than that she was a servant and needed to stay in her place, cradling his plates, and filling his water glass. So she rubbed his silverware and watched, always watched- as the two of them entertained each other each night. But the man observed her frustration and he was touched by it. *But does he feel the same way about me*, she thought. *Would she be forever ignored*? There had to be no hope.

Dinner concluded, and the wife returned to her bedroom and then to bed while the maid occupied her kitchen, when she then turned to plead to the man for some kind of recognition. In his eye was willful resignation. He approached. As he neared, he outstretched his arm and clasped her hand in the basin of dishwater. He longfully acted out the beginnings of what she had hoped would be just the two of them forever. He moved in close to her and, glancing quickly behind him for any prying eye of his wife, he placed his lips to hers and silenced any beginnings of speech. Her eyes dart away for secrecy and as they end their moment quickly, they share one last embrace with their glances, eliciting surrender. The man withdrew to his room and she retreated to her chamber again."

Sofia closed the book and the music continued until Albrecht got up to pour himself a draught and drank from its glass at his piano. She hurried back to her apartment to a night of sleepless anticipation.

8

There was time away from Albrecht's music and from his books. Sofia carried on the activities of living during the day and rehearsed by night. The pressures of work were overwhelming and she was unable to see through to the end. There she lay tossing and turning. Was there any light in the dark? Was there help on the way?

She lay remembering about the past, when Albrecht had played a performance at the Metropolitan

Museum of Art, and she had attended. She was one of only a few in the spacious performance hall. The first movement was an auditory manifesto of rebellion and personal conquest. She thought of herself his equal at her violin. Then she was taken away and subdued by a movement of Tchaikovsky. She had awaited the third movement and there he had made waves and gone head first into its complex expressions. She could not have predicted that. The performance was brief but moving. Afterward, he left the stage without appreciation or applause. She was hoping for more than her bow could express that night, as she nursed her sore ego with her strings and her viol and their voluntary manipulation. She matched his intensity with her play. She believed she was letting him see her, to spy on her in defense of her lies and their exhibition. Lies that she told herself in order to deny what she was feeling for him.

Later, when she had tucked away her woody instrument, she silently promised him in his absence that she would see him again. She fell asleep with the thought of old memories and new promises.

While Sofia was away concentrating on her music, Albrecht did not remain fixed. He had returned to the usual and mundane, and supplemented his moods with alcohol. When he met a neighbor in his building they discussed topics of military history, and after several weeks, he attracted the attention of another resident with his play. They walked the hall prolifically every day as the season slowly passed by.

9

It was July and Albrecht was tearing apart things in his apartment with an ill-natured mind. He was in doubt as to whether he had misplaced his precious prized recording. It was one which he had made himself at the academy and had been heard on the radio throughout the musical world. His shelf was emptied of its contents and cases were strewn on the floor but it was nowhere to be found. He became enraged, not knowing for what or for where or for when it became. It was gone. Remembering his neighbor, he acted without thinking, and he let down his guard, and flew down the hall. He approached the room and he forced the door open. Inside everything was organized and in its place. He moved immediately to the stereophonics and there he found a pile of CDs. He tore through the pile upending and dispensing them to the floor. The prize recording was nowhere to be found.

Albrecht returned to his room. He was pacing the floor. Sofia was there picking up the mess he had made. She thought she would use her presence to settle him down, so she did the usual thing and she picked up the book and lay on the couch. Albrecht was calmed momentarily at seeing her and he returned to his daily routine, almost forgetting the occurrence and the recording. Sofia began to read where she had left off.

"The wife of the miner had been at the house for a month. Now she was explaining to him her plans for the next.

"You know, the liberal democrats are meeting in the city this week and I have to be there to organize a lobby for the trade guilds," she said sharply. "Why can't you find the money you need to fix this drafty old place we call home. I have letters to write and papers to read and I don't want to waste that time fooling around with you."

There was no love in the man's eyes for her. No tone in his voice or an inclination of his head that indicated he cared or even included her as a reason for happiness. Their relationship was all flats and lacked all melody. The maid observed the woman he called his wife, and learned she was making a voyage up the coast and around the cape for a political event. The miner had been warmer to her for a very important reason. One that she hoped was an indication of he and his wife's separation.

Within days, the wife was away aboard ship, up the coast near Plymouth bound for London. The maid

attended her duties with care and without the bur-
den of the other woman's overbearing presence, even
though the marriage still existed."

10

"Once the man's clothes had been washed and his house had been cared for, the maid waited for him by the window. When he had returned from the mine, he felt the young woman was restless about something, so he took her down to the cellar, there to count bottles of wine. It was like sinking into fathomless water for her. She had never been allowed to wander so far. The cellar contained valuable money making bottles of riserva and apothic of much net worth. The man lit

his lamp and by the twists and the turns of the narrow-
est halls, he led her into a vault to see dusky and dark
colored glass bottles and their labels, each placed very
neatly. The man was placid and ambivalent toward the
woman. His words to her alone in that place while his
wife was away were to her an opportunity. She spoke
to him in hushed muted tones and her crusade for him
was rife with the refrain of an impending separation
of him and his wife.

There it was a chore and she lifted and she studied
labels and dusted off bottles and in extreme frustration,
until finally she reacted with rage and shattered his
precious delicate glass vessels on the cellar floor. The
man then answered this insolent behavior of hers, as
he called it, in a pitch that showed his disappointment,
and rushing at her, he took her wrist and he gripped it
tightly. She reacted again this time with equal dissat-
isfaction. He demanded that she remain behind and
clean up the glass and soak up the red wine. As she did

so, she was reminded of the flow from her body, which was straightforward and easy to understand; but what coursed and what pulsed in the man's hands and in his groin, in contrast to his temperament, was altogether confusing to her.

While the man pounded up the stairs, he couldn't cope with how he felt without making a final break with his wife. With time on his hands, the man asked for the attention of the maid as she came up the stairs to the kitchen and ladled her red hands with clean water. Finally he spoke softly saying, 'I want you and I to have something to eat in the dining room.' So he sat in the next room while she fried bacon and cut melon and on that night while his wife was away, he ate and she watched and she waited and he stared.

There was only time between them now as his wife was away for only two long days. If only they could take this dissonance to someplace else. Some other place in the house like the bedroom or even right there at the table. She got angry and he got hot and discordant and both were now headed in erotic directions. So he left food uneaten as he left from the table and went to the door and took off his shirt and he looked to her for what was the only thing on his mind. She flung herself down the hall and had not gotten to the room when he ripped off her smock and lifted up her skirt and cupped her round ass in his hand while draping her arm over his shoulder. He squeezed and he prised her cheeks apart and she heard a wet smack and he picked her up and they both came together in the hall with her feet not even touching the floor.

They lay on the bed in secrecy and seclusion and in enjoyment of thin wispy relief: his hand in her hair and her hand on his thigh, covered with an old fine sheet and wearing very little. There was whispering and there was touching with long, gentle brushing of hands and fingers on skin. Hours passed and the mood lingered. After a while, he eased over onto her and she turned and exposed her behind and he easily gave in and his hips made the motion again and again.

They lay in peace. There was no guilt or shame and there was only fine quiet contentment."

Sofia closed the book and the piano continued to play for this man Albrecht. It responded to his hands, and it answered his touch with beautiful tones and it was like an accompaniment to her new image of him as the miner. She was not the same beside him on his couch. Her blood flowed, her fingers ached, her heart throbbed. She lifted herself off of the couch and moved to the window and poured herself a drink while he only partially observed her with his eyes. She turned away, unable to face him, then after a glass of Lambrusco she glanced over her shoulder at him and when he quietly trailed off of his playing she took a position facing him. There was no more concern for the outside world. There was no more time to pass by. He left the piano and came to her and he was not smiling as she began undoing her blouse and he saw her as she truly was: naked underneath, carefully forgetting to have worn anything else beneath her blouse. They were together for no more than a minute when finally he turned to the piano. She retreated to his door and back to her room at the end of the hall.

11

Later that week, Sofia hurried from place to place, lighter without the weight of Albrecht's masculine potential. He was back at his keys cursing and swearing and not even hitting the right notes. On her icy couch down the hall Sofia sat in sequestration and she removed herself from all interference, and so secluded, she had some sense of all the different manners of being in love.

Albrecht was determined yet continually losing his way and stumbling through a fog of his past grievances with women.

The reenactment of forced manipulation of Sofia on her violin during practice was leading her down a path. One in which she placed her hand on herself in aggressive ways, and when she got home she performed for him in the mirror, in only a blouse, and when she had cum and not had enough she loped to her boudoir with untold lust.

Sofia had had this feeling many times before. It was the pain of something which Albrecht had no part in. So she traveled the length of the room to the closet to look and to find not just another fine dress. Nothing would rain down on her once the music began again.

Albrecht had had no more time for other commitment. He slept late and suffered a kind of dotage related to the wet dreams that nature forced on him in his sleep. The morning light was brighter and his vision was clear and it was frightening. He closed the shades. He threw dirty clothes in their own corner. There were full bottles and there were empty glasses and he filled one unclean glass and stood and palmed his forehead, seeking the peace of God as he drank. What about others? He had no time for that question and what it implied. Why not leave it to others to ruin his good name over the temptations of idolizing Sofia and the objectivity of her sex? What could he have done to her? What *should* he have done to her? What should he do next? These were the questions he asked himself but he could not communicate to her.

Sofia overcame his indecisiveness and she clung to him. And time passed. She had no other responsibilities, so she spent her time modeling her clothes for him, and she laid on his couch everyday, and he loved her for it. So much so that he pushed her away and down the hall and back to her room with words of regret or lack of attention to her, just so he could bring her back again with promises and with kisses and with pleadings. She couldn't help ever to change him. *He must not have been secure in his manhood*, she told him. So he retreated to his piano and she went back to her room, once again to her bow and she slung arrows at him from behind closed doors, until she was once again ready to open them to him, and let him watch her masturbate for him, after months of pouting and inflicting pain in the name of climax.

When finally he had agreed to see her, she returned to his room at the other end of the hall and wandered in and laid on the couch and opened up the book to where she had left off.

"Days passed and there was no sign of the wife. She had not returned from her congress or her journey to the city. The man looked at the maid and she looked at him. He would pace down the hall and she continued to keep the house in order for them both. She was in the midst of a problem. She could not stay and pretend and not demand it of him to end his marriage to his wife. Send either her or his wife away. She worked until her back hurt and she did it for him because he was all that much better for it and he treated her well and that was more important to her than anything else had ever been. But it was not enough. Then, seven days after the anticipated return of the wife, a letter arrived. It read:

The HMS Burgundian has gone down off the coast of Eastbourne. The search for survivors continues.

Because there was no looming danger on the horizon, the miner and the maid were safe for the foreseeable future, during which, the man made her a more valuable member of his household. More valuable than any of his most prized possessions. The search for survivors continued by day and by night and the young maid felt sorrowful and deserving of some fitting punishment. She felt defenseless yet bold, and most of all triumphant, because the wife had not been the man's happiness in life.

The maid lay powerless while the man walked the miles back and forth to the mine. She lay in his bed and tore away the sheets and they tangled her arms and legs as she fought for air. She fought also his pull and his weight and the swelling in her belly.

So too continued the business of the mine."

As Sofia closed the book, she realized that the man at his piano had provided her a life, but she clung to such a rocky and uncertain future, because of his drinking, his temperament and because of her own desire to be more than his valuable inanimate possession. And so she stayed for a while on his couch while she pondered the lines of his face, out of the blue, and into a shelter from an overwhelming and oppressive instinct to get pregnant.

She stayed until she realized that he only had per-formance on his mind then she rebounded and be-came herself again. She got up and walked the same hall much livelier than before, like once she had done in a school play. When she came down to the end, she returned to her apartment and shut and locked the door. *I've come this far already, and so I can't stop now*, she thought. She forbade herself the urge toward self loathing. That night she slept well.

12

The next day, she crawled onto his couch and into the book.

"There was a great rocky crag before the swale and it bore a great tumultuousness of waves, hurtling the timbers of the unfound ship now disintegrated, onto the rocks and into wooden splinters. There struggled the wife in the waves. Her only reaction to each hollowed swell and to each insurmountable peak, with their potential to batter and pummel her brains against the crag, was to flail with head, hands and foot. Without answer or rebuff the waves had continued their lashing. And the depth at its deepest was beyond hoping for a merciful drowning death. Still there was another conquest of wave, and she lost the fight not to breathe water during the light of the next day. So as the wife was reaching toward a flock of birds, Albrecht at his piano, at that moment of the opus, was, by chance, in the midst of expression of this woman at the verge of her death.

Along the street, and in the shop windows, faces were pale, lips were tremulous, and eyes were darting or were downcast. Thoughts of the fate of the HMS Burgundian were creating much anxiety. Out past the swale beyond the rocky shelf, the woody boats were searching in frantic anticipation of a life still clinging to its existence. The call of the search and the blare of the whistle, shrill and piercing, would be heard by anyone remaining but not yet found. Lanterns swayed in the night and by day bore no witness to anything living or dead. All had been swept away. Such was the destruction of the HMS Burgundian.

In the time that passed the housemaid was no more. She had been elevated to higher level of self. And through her anxieties, the spirituous affects of the wife still lingered. She could wait no longer. She had to make the next move.

But then there came a messenger and a letter to the door. He was plain and ambivalent. He thrust a brown envelope into the miner's hand. At the desk in the room where the business of the mine was kept, the man seized the letter and tore out its contents with a shaky hand. He unfolded it and delved deeply into it and he concluded its grisly and wonderful message:

No survivors had been found.

And then he wept for joy.

As the miner and his maiden donned their fur coats and wore their felt hats, and spent their fair share, he grew out his stubble and she let down her hair. They let the world go to ruin in cliché and explored the new lands in their domain."

Sofia closed the book while Albrecht at his piano was in the pursuit of his *Eroica*. So she sat anxiously awaiting him to discover her at this erotic threshold: of being on the verge of this happiness with him being her beau. She wanted him to notice her again, so she got up from his couch and she acted out the part of a knave, or of a maid; organizing and caring for his strewn about books, all in the expanse of an hour in the afternoon; but when he took no notice, only telling her to leave well enough alone because he didn't want a domestic after all, she left him with his thoughts and returned to her place at the end of the hall.

13

Albrecht took one look at himself in the mirror after an intense night of strategizing and he decided that she was meant for him. Why else had this diplomated, fine young woman from down the hall taken up his couch and done nothing but read his romance novels, and dust his books? He had come up with a plan. He would take his best bottle of shiraz and he would go to see her and she would lead him into another beautiful paradigm.

When Sofia had heard his knock at the door and she had let him in, he unsheathed his bottle of wine.

She turned down his drink because suddenly her need to be pregnant resurfaced, and without batting an eye, he emptied his glass into the sink, and captivated her with his smile instead. So she let down a shoulder strap and she pried at his groin with her one hand, signalling him to act. He removed a latex condom from his pocket and she took it from his hand and threw it in the trash, and when she had finished with him on her knees instead, she chased it with a glass of wine, and spit it out into the sink. When he was ready again, she fought back a tear and rode him down on his back. By the morning there was no more fear of equivocation.

Sofia rose early and woke Albrecht as she escaped from the bed. She went to make coffee and he dressed in the previous night's clothes that were there in a pile on the floor by the bed. He used the facilities, then sat in the nook and drank a cup of it black while Sofia held his free hand there resting on the table. It was a moment for neglecting all else.

He exited not only the room but then the front door after exchanging glances with Sofia one last time, and returned to his keep.

After that, Albrecht was struck with great lucidity in his play and in his thoughts. It was difficult for him to find fault with her, but he left her alone for a time, seeing only his piano and his books and his recordings. He had been in a using mood, and now at a fast pace he removed impurities from his mind again, and from his apartment, which he made all very neat. He avoided contacting her for weeks.

Once Sofia knew she was pregnant, she packed her cello and viol and violin, and boxed up her wardrobe, then left her furnished apartment promptly thereafter, leaving the musical world behind and making a course for far away with the thoughts of motherhood and its challenges to her body and mind.

When Albrecht had finally returned to discuss what had happened between them, she had already gone. He thought he had done something for her, but maybe he had imagined it. He thought maybe it had been temporary, and now she was getting away. He had fears but he also had desires and now he was left without a woman again. She had been a one night stand like all of the rest. He was staring into a grim future of misunderstanding and lonely death, he was certain.

14

Sofia left the crowded cosmopolitan city behind for a new life raising her son, but she was not prepared for the challenges of single motherhood and its economic hardships.

She had been accustomed to a culture of art and music. Now she laid plans for a Midwestern heartland town awash in industrial grays and browns and surrounded by farmland.

There was no refinement or sophistication in the terms that she was used to. This was hard-working blue collar pride in the form of unions and pickup trucks. Her business was putting food on the table for her son, and at first it came in the form of a waitress uniform. She sold her instruments but kept her Stradivarius, no one knows why. Perhaps she was planning for emergencies or for the boy's graduation or simply intending it as a trust to him should something happen to her. She had been celebrated as a musician but now she was withdrawing from the money and privilege which that provided, but never from effort. Her hard work would continue and that was how she wanted it.

So for years she collected tips in roadside cafes and rented a small unit in a quiet neighborhood within walking distance of a school. Her job and her life were filled with strange new people with hidden pasts and dark desires. She worked the endless hours to avoid their invitations and came home alone until she became familiar with the regular customers and the wayfarers and simply the customers who were curious about her.

Her job was not her strong suit. She fumbled at the register and argued with the other staff and she dismissed the cook as a chauvinist. Being on her feet endless hours was causing her back pain, and the schedule between home and work was cutting into her sleep time.

Barely coping at work and in great need of spending money, Sofia met with a man who gave her a rose and asked her to visit with him at a place not far from where she worked. She gave him the invitation to her place instead, for reasons of safety. He said there was no one on his mind or in his life but the possibility of her, and she said the same. The significance for her was that he was moving in on what had been Albrecht's domain, and she knew it, but she satisfied his crazy demands anyway, and it was not kinky, just sex and nothing more. He paid and left and she showered and removed the dirty sheets from the bed and then she turned her focus to where the real activity was. At the corner, she exchanged the money for merchandise and she satisfied her not really so frequent drug urge.

She had given up her musical career for the benefit of her son. On a daily basis she was confronted with her own duality: a moral depravation and a desire to make ends meet, but she could scarcely believe it was not just some passing dream in the night that she cleaned up after in the morning. The image repeated itself day after day over the course of several years, if she needed money for her son's happiness.

"Hold me closer," she would say. "Your effforts won't go unrewarded."

Then, when the strange man had gripped her tightly, and she without flinching was very still, they fuck. Immediately after, she would press him for money and then see him off again, into his night life.

15

Far away, Albrecht was receiving offers to record albums on the other side of the ocean.

His conquest of England began with the Grammaphone Recording Company. It was old and dusty music. They were the greatest classics, and with them he perfected the clavier. The company believed in him and he was supremely confident in that trust. So he moved into a flat in York and he began a life of ease and a one of betrayal. It was a type of celebrity status. All the while he had not forgotten that he had left someone behind. For the time being, however, he remained level-headed, yet always in danger of falling short of social standards.

The studios at the Grammaphone Company were within walking distance of his flat and he had other flats, also in Dusseldorf and Vienna. He always allowed his driver to shuttle him to and from his places of work and recreation.

York, England was an urban center built on the remnants of an old establishment settled by Norse invaders. They had come down from Denmark and offenced all the Saxons who had civilized the kingdoms of Mercia, Umbria and Wessex. That was also an old and dusty classic lore. His flat was on High Street where the Dane Law had left its mark on history. His room was down at the end of the hall with a window overlooking the gray of the wharf. Outside and surrounding the flat were the canals and the districts of commercial trade, but his flat in relation to the wharf was separate and distinct.

He brought his Fabbrini and his books and his Audi, which his driver had fair control over. This excursion into England was just a matriculation into what he had begun at the academy. He had brought memory of it, and of the woman at the end of the hall, who had sat and read on his couch. But she had never told him that his love had given them a son. He had to find that out much, much later and it had not had the deprecating effect that it had had on her, nor alter his life in any way, before she would eventually return to him.

He sometimes played for British royalty in the Admiralty Hall, and for that he was lavished and set apart. But he grew disputatious and had a reputation for bickering about the media. He read about himself in profile, and in interviews in newspapers and magazines. But because he didn't like what was said in them, he crooned about image and proprieties as he flew back and forth in his flat, often stopping to loaf about, dusting his books, which would divert his attention away from his piano. When he'd revert back to playing, he brought back his interpretation, now older in form, and he perfected a worldly stroke. He was capricious and foolhardy but also very symmetrical. He became more temperamental as time passed and he was someone quite multidimensional.

He missed the woman at his couch. He missed Sofia. He missed the modeler of clothes, the reader of books, and the admirer of his music. He missed the fuck of his life. He'd had her when he had wanted her, and she'd given him no reason to look around for other women, and still he had wanted more from her.

16

Albrecht traveled to Germany and in Dusseldorf he recorded another album for Grammaphone. In Dusseldorf, the air was clean, and the city was punctuated with black tile, a ferris wheel and a river. The city became a leader in electronic music very nearly the same time that Grammaphone considered using Albrecht to revive Classical music there among the intelligentsia.

Albrecht was sleepless and depressed when he met a contemporaneous young performer there named Marie, a pianist like himself, and they played a concerto for two pianos as part of a promotion for Grammaphone. It was well received by the educated and elite.

When Albrecht and Marie practiced together, she kept him moving and she kept him guessing and he wished he could run off with her at their very first moments alone. Though he was a polisher of dusty old classics, she found him to be quite sophisticated, is how she put it, and not so genteel- but tall, lazy and weak. Just what about that she liked, she never said. Ostensibly, she was straight, but he had his retinue who were always colluding, and that made her nervous and unsure of herself.

Her career had more than the expectation that Albrecht's had and because she was young and she was German she was a national symbol. But she was wild and free, owing to the common knowledge that her teachers had been Ferrari and Volvo. She ate like a horse, and she liked to make lists and she drank out of short, squatty glasses which were tinted like the crystal clear blue of her almond eyes. When she wore a sleeveless at Albrecht's Fabbrini, her arms were pricked with pink and pulsating with life and always in motion like her bouncing breasts, where there was always a nipple in relief of its blouse, protruding.

Before they met, Marie thought Albrecht would walk by without seeing her. But in fact, he couldn't take his eyes off of her.

At first there had been glances in different directions. She would look to one side and he would look to the other. First left then right. Her eyes floated to the ceiling, not really looking at anything at all. He took a quick look at her breasts then looked away. Their eyes met. He complemented her features: her looks, her face. She was warmed by that. Then he threw his eyes in her direction and undid her defenses with a look that opened a door. He threw a clutch from her reach and she was without means to retaliate. So he opened up a barrage of questions at her, and she jumped all over it gregariously. He demanded to know the when and the where and the why. Then he launched into his statements of, "I" this and "I" that. The alcohol had helped relax their perturbations.

They could have been anywhere for all time, and they hit it off with acquiescences. "Yes," he agreed and, "I thought so too," she said. And then she picked him up in her Volvo and she took him to the bibliotecha, and there they debated their chemistry. They glossed over the tough answers to the tough questions, and there were no communication problems just yet. So he went home without his sunglasses because he left them in her car for an excuse to bring her back again.

Marie called him and told him that he had been careless to forget them, and then laughed. He said they were worthless, goading, and she said not to be silly and told him she would be over to drop them off. She sped down the autobahn, to his open door, and his waiting arms (she was not upset to discover) but since she was unsure of herself, she simply returned his belongings and left. Perhaps she doubted him or questioned his motives, or simply disregarded his efforts. Maybe she was in love with what she thought she was accomplishing, but it was nothing at all according to him. She was still advancing without achieving anything, and happy just to display her tush, while at night she curled up in a ball and slept in the cold because of loneliness.

When Albrecht felt as though his name and his reputation were being passed off publicly from hand to hand shamelessly and indefinitely without either exhaustion or achievement of love, like just so much currency, he paid Marie's fare and brought her back in a taxi, because he didn't want her driving away again.

She arrived at his new address, temporary and furnished, and she was willing to climb stairs to his door, and she entered in.

Her eyes were focused with energy and they vibrated with life, and though he was weak and lazy he could support her with one arm and palm her rear end with one large hand.

So he slivered some almonds with a razor blade, and made a cranberry marmalade and drank an espresso because it was the thing to do there, and because he had brought her there to pamper her. He set a place for her and he bathed her and slept with her, and she felt as though she were running into the arms of her father or as into some safe haven. After they had coerced each other playfully, he would lift up one fine breast, and tickle her calf, and when he did, she observed always his hands with her skin. Sometimes majestic and royal, cool and white, and sometimes nubile and natal, and sometimes the right hand between her legs was very dispassionate and not achieving anything for either one of them. But when they did it his way, he would perform like a Beethoven symphony, only using her hand on him in the dark when he was too shy for sex. She liked him so much at that point that she shared his place in Dusseldorf much of the time, and they kept it stocked with flowers.

17

Marie noticed many spare pairs of things in Albrecht's flat. There while he played and then when he was not, she tried on his vast amounts of clothes in grays and in browns and put on his shirts and relaxed in his boxers and she went barefoot. She tried on the spare things and the sleeveless tops too small for him and why he had them, she didn't care to ask. They had all been folded neatly with darker clothes on top so as not to disturb his eyes. She looked good in his clothes and she knew it.

She walked so much in his apartment, she seemed to be pushing the boundaries of a nomad. Her range for that was indeed global and foretelling. Every day she prayed for the rain never to stop shutting them in.

When he went to see her at her place, and she was not there, he became frantic. There was a pattern of women leaving him at all the wrong times, during all his moments of surrender to them. He couldn't forego or forsake her, but his quest for love was a vacuous interpretation of some misplaced sentiment. He found that he needed her approval to feel sadness, and he was sure she was keeping him on a hook and hanging him out to dry.

He slammed the doors and he broke off the hinges. He shattered the glass and threw the forks and spoons and he upended the table to the floor. He felt no muscular strength in any of that. He wanted her in the air and in the bedroom and in the mind. It is *all* temporary, Marie, he imagined himself telling her, in the case he had been the promotion of just some fling from her.

So he pulled apart a mango after his violent convulsions had ended, and his ego suffered violently also. Afterward, he took his taurine, and his omegas, and his selenium and prepared for yet another day of heartless sustaining misery. Marie was in demand somewhere and he wished she would make herself unavailable to whoever they were for his sake and for the sake of their memories together. He survived but he was not living. He returned to nothingness again, where everything went on without him. He returned to his piano to create some stir like a witch's brew, so the winds and the demons would set the people in motion again.

When Marie finally returned, she looked every bit the part of the wild Irish rover, with wandering eyes and combative energy.

Albrecht was not amused by the mood she was in. What kind of end would she achieve out of shaming herself? Wouldn't she want a better part to play? He didn't want to make a child's game out of it. Why calm down? She made him happy; and hot at other moments as well. Maybe she was just leading him on. He needed to confuse her. Lead her with his impulse. Like the deep bass of lower instinct. Maybe he should swing on a vine for her. The sonnets of love mention only birds in the trees. Should she climb the vine, she would find him where he was the legend of Greystoke. Musculatory as he would never be unfortunately. And should she fall, he would catch her. All the expressions in one. No solo would do. It would have to be a pair of voices.

And the most ironic thing happened next.

18

Outside of the adventures of the men and of the drugs, Sofia began to see the disadvantages of being separated from her music, from Albrecht and his piano and the prospect of telling him she'd given him a son. It had been a mistake to think that she could do this on her own. She thought about the ways of seeking him out and asking him for the money to continue to raise their son and to spoil him and to prevent him from seeing another bad influence. Her independence had not been secure or steady or predictable. It had its moments but they were enslaving her to their habitude and the evil attributes of addictions. And always others had become very judgmental. Therefore, with the prospect of ill conscience now raining down insults on her, she rang Albrecht in Germany and gave him the news she'd withheld for so long. At hearing this, he became overjoyed and he made arrangements that brought her out of necessity and into luxury.

Traveling to Germany was like returning home to her room at the end of the hall and visiting him at his end once again. The years had left their mark and were like a tremendous weight on her because of their experiences together long ago. It was now becoming more apparent when returning once again.

She wondered whether there was truth to his joy and sincerity behind his support, since she had kept this from him for so long, or whether he would lecture and be gravid or whether he would be sentimental. He was ten years older than the older man he was when they met. She slumped in her seat wondering if he would share with her that flame once again. Would it resume or would she have to rekindle it?

Albrecht made arrangements for Sofia to stay in York, beyond the wharf but not so near because he was not ready to wash away ten years of separation and silence. She had expected him to see his boy but he had given her means to send him to boarding school for the time being. When the time came, Sofia and Albrecht met the boy in Edinburgh after traveling separately to see him at his lesser academy there in the city of Seven Hills between Pentland and the Firth. They took a trip to the public lyceum where their son would someday be attending public lectures in preparation for a conservatory, if he did well enough.

19

He should have told Marie that it was just physical between he and Sofia. However, he was weakened by the pull of old times, and because of that he brought Marie down with him, so he pleaded to her for her understanding.

"Its simpler doing things my way, Marie."

"It can't always go your way, Albrecht."

"The world won't ever be just one way, Marie."

He wanted to seduce her once again, but she wanted him to know himself better.

"It's not my job to know what you want," she said as though she was proclaiming her innocence.

He decided that he would put an obstacle in her path. He would insert the role of Sofia. And so, without thinking, he approached Marie, and he expressed his need for Sofia, and she didn't know what to say or think, so she put on an air of superiority and disgust.

The first time Sofia met Marie, she had been in his flat and sitting on his couch. There was some cute young woman occupying what had once been her domain. But there had been time between them. How could she have expected anything else different? Albrecht had never bothered to introduce them. *He has faults*, Sofia thought. She stumbled around the flat between the dusty old books and she finally drew the young woman into conversation. But it was dull and impotent discussion. When their meeting was over,

Sofia's goodbyes were concealing her true nature as was *le bisé*, and her arm around the young woman's shoulders, abjectly, and she was not so certain if she'd ever be back.

The second time they'd met it had been torment. Sofia wore a cloak. One that was a loosely worn charade of giggling and snickering fun with the guile of felicity, because in the phony enthusiasm for their short personal history together as musicians (though she'd had her suspicions) she was equally jealous of their musical connection. But it was Marie that would set the wheels in motion.

20

Albrecht got into his car and drove out past Manchester. A sign was posted, beyond the comfortable settings in between the market district and organized rows of townhouses. It signalled a different place. It was the end of reliable communication and the flows of commerce. Albrecht's Audi took an alley during the later part of the afternoon from the flats at the low end of town. The region was well known for its greed, wide canals and its red light deeds. As he drove angrily through the avenues lined with crowds of weekend celebrants, Albrecht made a new observation. The outrant development was no less attractive than the geography beyond the signs and posted warnings. The place where he was going was a distraction from the pressures afforded his life. So he drove away from the internment of being needy in a controversial period in his life, to where the pubs and the furniture stores and restaurants boasted of the twenty somethings who portrayed their personalities in strange and charming ways. As he looked at the faces, he could remember much of Sofia. He glanced to his left where a group of students were sporting beads and laughing, all gay and drunk, and he wondered if they came from up-town. He drove with speed and while tightening his automotive gloves and shifting the transmission with his left hand, he sped farther beyond that place, and then it began to rain. The rain elicited false conclusions from his mind. He drove toward a gray sky, and what seemed like well beyond the last spacious development rife with swimming pools and wooden fences. Beyond the memory of Sofia. His Audi made time in the small foothills and the horizon opened up. He read the names, Carmarthen and Pembrokeshire. The nearest new path was Conwy, at ten kilometers, so he signaled and veered.

21

After Albrecht had left for a drive, Marie undid the latch and let in a person of reputation such as Sofia, with the intent to look at his books and lay on the couch together. Sofia knew she was invading some dream of his, and she wanted it to be known that she was in it too. She decided she would let Marie take her wherever she wanted to go, but she would not let her make the mistakes of naivety.

She began simply with the admission of her bi-sexuality, asking Marie only if she was curious also at some point in her life, then letting the subject go. And then, after a session of play, she majestically descended from the shower, naked in front of the bold yet cautious Marie.

Marie was instantly aroused, and jealous of the future being in the body of Sofia. She wanted to put hands on her there and then, and instead she guided Sofia's hands to her private parts as Sofia very smoothly and handsomely, skillfully and proficiently obliged.

Sofia and Marie never stopped to ask what was right. Or for forgiveness. They only defied their limitations for physical and emotional completeness.

Marie had no regrets, and though she had thought about Albrecht within the beginnings of a relationship with Sofia, she still could not replace him in her imagination.

They were bathed and scented and they were alone together and it was after hours. Sofia turned down the sheets and dimmed the light, while Marie relaxed on the bed.

Sofia touched Marie's hand. She pressed her lips. She slid a leg between hers.

"Be forever near to me and I promise you the world, Marie."

And they made love. Days passed with devotion to the secrecy of Marie's prodigiousness at experimentation with Sofia and same sex love.

With all the experiences of Dusseldorf which Sofia tried her best to surpass in love for Marie, she brought her into her stay and she cooked. She provided numerous and sumptuous ladles of thick, classic ragu and a table full of unbroken noodles of every kind with dices of German sausages, where they could and did twirl it up with their forks, down to the emptiness of their plates and the fullness of their bellies.

After spaghetti they vied for the upper hand but neither could climb out of their entanglement long enough to resist.

Again and again and Marie fell into the trap.

Sofia looked at Marie with penetrating eyes, and she beckoned her,

"Come away with me my love and we will go to Vienna where we will play together, just you and I, and we will be an inseparable pair, the world at your feet and roses in your hair." And so Marie accepted the lure of Sofia and they were born away to Vienna, together.

22

The Viennese lounged idly by the Danube, despite the brisk November morning. Tourists filled with wanderlust shuffled expectantly between Schonbrunn and Hofburg. Though the Hapsburgs had since retired their rule, four hundred years of the stone parapets of palaces had made pirouette in front of the many neighboring villas beside the wide river. Along the filigree and beneath the apse, whose patronage was the patrimony of medieval emigré into the Holy Roman

Empire, liberal cosmopolitan millennials sat and contemplated their city. The coffee was Turkish, by tradition, and Sofia and Marie pondered the rebuilding of an opera house blown apart by a savage world conflict eighty years since gone by, passing not without thought, as the cargo passing back and forth across the Danube to places like Asia minor. It was, by means of the terrible Nazis, that a tapestry of diaspora was murderously rent apart from Austria and thrown into the fire, and because of that the city had never forgotten its character or its diversity.

The pair of lovebirds lay roost in a vitreous sublet carved out of many rooms and many spaces filled with light. There were adjoining bedrooms with portes-fenetres rising up from wooden floors. It was a boon of secrecy from the outside world where their popularity as revered musicians of much renown kept the authorities searching.

In Vienna, Sofia perfected a disguise, and she continued her recitals with the young *paramour* under a false pretense.

Sofia instructed Marie not to sit so straightly, with suggestive statements that she embellished with a beautiful voice and with motherly sounds, and she allowed her to play uninterrupted. She not only complemented her with her violin and with colorful notes like vocal responses, she deflected her concentration into that space with excessive hyperbole of heaven and hell and death and the devil and they played other things that made fantasy in every direction, somehow somewhat completely unfinished.

Sofia evoked in Marie a feeling not unlike a wide open room with opportunity in every direction, drawing her in. The woman offered her something complementary and glittering with romantic preference. Without demand or authority, it was not statutory or competitive.

During the times that Sofia thought of Albrecht, she went deeply into *a danse sensuelle* and she wooed and she seduced his *protégée* and she established the bounds of love and desire and she accomplished this with nuance and suggestion and always the temptations of her bedroom.

The rhythm of the strings of an oud made a chilling complement to the sessions of lovemaking between Sofia and Marie. As charming as she was dominating over Marie's untamed impulses for her own sex, she stopped at nothing but that, and Marie was not incontrovertible in the end.

23

"What have you to say about it all?" Sofia asked Marie.

"That I like it here and I'm falling for you and it may not be just a passing thing." replied Marie.

So Marie called Albrecht and there she had words of small betrayal.

"Where have you been?" he asked without astonishment.

"I've been away with Sofia."

"Have you thought about me? Are you angry with me?"

"I'm trapped. I love Sofia and I love you."

"How could that be?" asked Albrecht as he was seeing the failure of his attempt to bring Marie closer to him.

"You were the one who brought us together. Now tell me what I am supposed to do about it," pleaded Marie.

"Yes it was me, Marie. But now you should return to what you and I had before."

Albrecht thought and he agonized and he meted out judgment. He blamed Sofia for her unrelenting instinct and for her intrusion. And he blamed Marie for her own incipient and jejune nature. She was inexperienced and he had put her in a vulnerable position and she had taken the bait and had used it to induce the jealousy he now felt. *Had she meant that all along?*

He must now tear her away from Sofia, if there was to be any future. So he rung Sofia at home.

"So what are you doing with Marie then, Sofia?" demanded Albrecht.

"Sharing in your dreams Albrecht. Dreams that had once been the two of ours."

"You shouldn't have taken Marie from me Sofia, but now what do you intend to do about her."

"Why, do you miss her? Do you miss me? is she special to you? Aren't I ?"

"Leave her. I only wanted to make her want me more."

"At a price."

"What do you mean?"

"I want more, also, Albrecht."

"Go on."

"I want three million Euros."

"And then?"

"And then I slap her and I send her back to you, with her tail between her legs. And know this Albrecht, I may succeed in sending her to you, but she will not go willingly. She may never see your side again, now that she's fallen in love with me. I hope you're prepared for that."

"She wasn't yours to take, you know."

"She was no good for you and now she's nothing to me."

So Albrecht bought out Sofia for the right to see Marie, and with the consolation of an endowment, or rather a sinister payoff, Sofia had to break her bond with Marie and in the worst way possible. A way that would satisfy Albrecht, and join the two of them again, like a dove's tail.

So Sofia approached Marie as they stood staring out of the window in their room in Vienna.

"I'm sorry, I dont know how to tell you. Albrecht demands we put an end to this, to us. He says we are having an affair." She undid Marie with that comment.

"You said he meant *nothing* to you."

"Thats what you thought. He's been keeping tabs on you. He's been keeping tabs on us both."

Marie argued again and again.

"Look, Marie. I've had you and now I'm done with you. You're nothing to me after all. I only made love to you because I thought it would make Albrecht jealous. You don't love Albrecht as I do and I can see it in your eyes."

Marie left the room and left Sofia, turning to look at her in her pitiful moment of forfeit and resignation, as though a decision had been made for her. She wondered then whether it would be Sofia whom Albrecht would return to.

Marie was torn from reason, and lived in an alternate reality for a long time afterward. She survived but didn't live. She played music. The music of memory. *Her* piano. Marie recalled the words of Sofia. *You don't love Albrecht. I can see it in your eyes*. Why had she told her that?

She searched her feelings for Albrecht. She found him in her heart. But did it feel like she wanted it to? If it didn't flutter, it didn't amount to anything. She would have to confront him again to know the meaning of what lie in her heart.

24

Albrecht was in a new apartment now. It had problems, including its emptiness without either woman. Tenancy was down, neighbors were loud and the car traffic was ceaseless. Darkness prevailed. There was misery in his abandonment at Sofia's hand. There must be something much more desirable left to discover. She had been unfair to him and Marie both. Handn't she made her decision to be without him in the beginning? She hadn't had explanation enough for what should have been better for the both them but turned out so poorly for her and so lonely for him. He had only been heeding his instincts and she'd had what she cared about. *Why had she turned her attention toward Marie anyway?* He knew she had needed money but why had she stopped her career to begin with? The rain in Dusseldorf continued. A reign of sadness. He thought of Marie again. Maybe it was because Marie had wanted to see herself from behind someone else's eyes. But he would have been forever sad that he would not have been that other lover. He had seen her for some time before she had gone missing with Sofia. She had sounded accusatory to him when she had rung him from Vienna. *Why did you lead me to this woman?* She had asked. *Is it a part of some plan to destroy yourself?* When he had learned of Sofia's manipulation of them both to reestablish her relationship with him and begin again her career, he hadn't made Marie see her for who she was. And then Marie seemed as though she was ready to end it all, even her life. If she rebounded, what about their future? He knew that she loved Sofia but would she continue to love him?

25

"There must be a great gallantry of wrongs going on because no one wants to be used for your own selfish purposes anymore. I must admit that I have been interested in you in the same way as Sofia, but you don't have to be heartless anymore to do that for me." said Marie.

"What do you mean by heartless?" asked Albrecht.

"Giving mine to other people." stated Marie.

"I would still consider you mine even if you were to have time for others." said Albrecht.

"Now that I'm done with Sofia what will you do next?" She thought out loud.

It was Albrecht who had introduced Marie to her sexual captivity. Love and music had only increased that desire. Albrecht had signaled to her that she was not ready for anyone else yet. It had been the voice of reason and of God. He had wanted Marie to see Sofia as a whore, but Marie had wanted him to see *her* as someone like that. *Why had he not thought of her that way before?* In the end, however, she was glad he had given her a part to play.

Marie returned to Albrecht but there was a gulf between them. Neither realized the result of her tryst.

"How did you carry on like that without *me*? And for what result? Did you think I really meant it if I ever said you wouldn't ever be here with me again?" asked Albrecht.

"No." said Marie meekly.

"Do you wish there was something else?"

"No one other than you anymore." said Marie. She was beyond reminding him of his attachment to Sofia, and struggling to make sense of his love for her.

"Say what you really mean." said Albrecht.

"How did you ever lose me?" asked Marie.

"I'm telling you that was the past and your thing with Sofia was an expression of my love for you and not for her."

"But she took me in when you couldn't." said Marie.

"Forget about her. You're mine now and always. For all time's sake."

She was glad he said that, and glad that he was still interested in her in that way even if it was not for the purposes of his creativity. But there was a problem with it, and there needed to be a beginning, because it seemed to them like they had always existed only for the service of others, as the servants of music.

So Albrecht reached out to Marie and held her close and he whispered,

"Be devoted to me Marie, and I will take you beyond the boundaries of love and desire and into a rapturous existence of the world around us."

She consented, saying, "Yes truly, I will."

As they lay together on the bed, Albrecht listened to the cries of an oboe and its tale, while he watched the lights flicker and play on the white milky skin of her back, bare on the bed on the avenue of sleep. The sound of the oboe was like the sound of a morning mist in a green valley, where he teetered on the edge of sanity once again.

26

Ashamed of not only the past, but hopeful for better news, Sofia separated the miles from the years, and she connected with her son at his request. She was in need of that kind of attention and at that time she understood his father again, and then her own father, as if that same man had played both roles.

So with the past behind her, and the money turning every head toward her while satisfying her every need, Sofia entered the English Oak Room one fortunate weekend. It was nestled in the corner of the lower floor of a large walking space under a equally impressive glass roof. On her way to dinner at the Oak Room she passed the benignly swaying palms, and the pulsing fountains and the marble staircases, winding into the upper reaches. She was unencumbered, and free and not tied down by anything or anyone.

On that one particular night, she drifted over her soup and sandwich, unharassed by any thoughts of culpability, when a man at the counter paid for his dinner and took his ticket number to display at his table. He set his number near the edge and proceeded to delve into his leather folio for some coffee-stained, rumpled papers torn from a legal pad.

He looked to be in his thirties, and he was covered in stubble and wore a corduroy suit coat. He extracted his wire frame glasses from his breast pocket and put them on the bridge of his nose.

He looked the part of security and stability albeit very threadbare. She watched him until her soup got cold and then she dunked a crispy crust into it. She watched him blot his sweating forehead with a napkin. He would often stare out of the window for someone who never arrived. And she watched him intently until she finished her sandwich and bought another, in order to continue to watch him.

His supper came, and though with all the gusto that the waiter provided, the man seemed uninterested in anything but his paperwork.

Suddenly, in walked a man, apparently unannounced. No identification was necessary. A thin face, long dark hair and three days of stubble coupled with the overabundance of black leather gave her discomfort and she reduced herself to a helpless child at her table.

There could be no other explanation for him and his aura other than the assurance that he was rebellious, dangerous, and in trouble with the law.

In truth, those in his circle were cutthroats. They were loyal only to each other. Their virtues were survival. They were not men of honor. But this man in black leather was different. He was the spoils. He smacked of defiance and of fight. Sofia saw all of that.

He was brusque and was cool and he brought a lot of heat and he shook his audacious mane and he looked slack and confined and piercing all at once.

The two men spoke in a harsh manner and they punctuated with their hands. Once their meeting concluded, the rebel sat and looked not the part of the Oak Room.

Sofia had been unsure of her emotions surrounding Albrect and Marie, so now she buried them deep inside of her and resolved herself to the notion of creating the perfect image of the man in the Oak Room. She met him that night when his lawyer had left and he was alone. She kept nothing from him, and he answered her questions and was up front and forward.

"What kind of trouble are you in?" she asked.

"Nothing money can't fix." Klaus said.

"I have plenty of that."

"So what do you want?" asked Klaus.

"I want you."

27

They hit it off, and it wasn't careless or innocent. There would be no confessions. There would have been no absolution, or acquittal. Klaus was her doll and she dressed him with care and with fuss. She stylized his apparel and his vestments down to his jockeys in brief and boxer, all cut, pressed, and rolled from the best silk.

She thought about him tall and thought about him flat on his back and she liked it like that. She thought about it long, hard and deep, slow and easy.

They were easy going and they were joined at the hip.

When she took him out he wore his dyed baby blue Nuovo unbuttoned at the cuffs. The black car that drove them being sleek and turbo should take them wherever there was to go, the driver said to the pair. And so they slid into the casino, and she taught him baccarat and to play with a nine, and to risk it without holding back. And they drank endless drinks served on silver trays and there they sat hand in hand. The whore that Sofia had been was long dead now that they carried the flame of their hidden cachot.

Now, newly identified by every strange passerby as an inviolate unweariness of the two of them, they turned every head and gained the attentions of all others, on whose lips were the words, "there goes money as no object."

Sofia often went back and forth to the Oak Room to dine alone, descending the marble staircase and lilting through the mall.

Maybe Klaus was reaching out to her deep in her subconscious without the physical responses of her replies. She imagined him in descending notes though she was surrounded by his voice on all sides of her in that enclosed walking space. He resonated something not acute, but wide and broad and it echoed like a bass drum at the bottom of the ocean or in some fluid filled chamber. But for now he was talking only to himself. He answered his own cries with his own responses in descending scales and in lower diapason, while she leered to one side or the other as a ship heavy with cargo, falls into the hollow of a wave. She had difficulty staying steady.

So she returned to her spacious enclave and stripped bare her thirty something frame and took out her violin and began to play in the lower reaches of the mind. She penetrated her ego with his masculinity and drew him in. She second-guessed his next appearance because she had him at knife's edge and his response would be either cowardice or bravery.

28

When Klaus met Sofia that weekend she made herself out to be a teenage dream to him. They roamed her mansion by candlelight after a walk through the woods and came to one of many empty rooms. He leaned into her for a kiss and when he did she reared up with her behind. So he grabbed her butt and undid the zipper of her jeans, and when he had exposed her pubic hair he began to massage her pussy slowly and firmly and then again softly and gently. He went down on her on the divan.

She climaxed and flooded his mouth with her essence and he liked it like that. When they were finished they rested side by side until he finally came to rest with her head on his chest.

He left satisfied and without plans for anyone else.

Without him she explored the cupboards, the closets and pretended she could see him there and sensed his movements. She wore only her oldest most comfortable clothes, and she blended into a dark, somber atmosphere, until he returned expecting more.

He massaged her pussy with his lips and mouth for several days on end until she was ready to move onto something else. She wanted to taste his cum.

So when he had been in the shower just briefly, she stole away his Nuovo from the hook behind the door and the silken boxers from the rack on the wall and she hid them on the floor of the entrance to her room, so that when he had left the bathroom shower looking for his clothes, he found her on her bed naked above the waist and eyeing him at the door as he stood there with a towel draped over his shoulder. Unable to fight back the impulse, his cock stiffened and stood, and he sidled into the room and she made space for him on the bed. She descended to his waist and she lay on his leg with her head there on his hip and she massaged his hairy pouch with her left hand, and then moving it to his hard member, she fingered the head and rubbed it down below and between it and his shaft, then she loosely gripped it and stroked it slowly and in short strokes. She observed its underside and she smoothed it onto her cheeks and the fore of her face and her lips, round and round, until it was vibrating so hard she thought she would split it two. She kissed it lengthily and softly over and over from the tip and the back and the top and the front and she looked away from his eye and stared down on it. She teased it into her mouth with her round full lips so slowly that he thought he would never cum. Her head twisted round slowly while she slid it in down to his sack and she followed the motion until she had it just so. He got up on his hands and he flexed his muscles and he came in her mouth with a tortured exhale. Each spurt of cum welled in her mouth and she swallowed it all at once at the end. She tasted every second of it. She knew it by its salt and its sugar and she remembered it like it was new again.

29

They did however attract attention. Unwanted attention. The wrong attention.

"If it wasn't for those standups, we would have it like you and me should, and it would just be about us," said the woman.

"Standups like who?" asked the man.

"Like that rich bitch and her man and that." she said.

"So what do we do about it?"

"We watch her, and when we're ready we make our move."

Klaus and Sofia occupied themselves at the bacarat table with their usual high stakes, amidst the fervor of a winning night at the casino.

Having seen Sofia with her man and knowing himself to be an opportunist, the patient and observant derelict went swiftly from the craps table and hurried back to her mansion where she kept her goodies. He trespassed there and had means to break in and put an end to her pompousness. So he crept without light and he knelt and he crawled until he had cracked every door and picked every lock and finding nothing available to hock he lit one and only one candle and crept up the stairs, knowing the house to be without occupant. He ransacked the upper floors and when he found what it was that brought him great pride, he snatched it up with its box and it fit neatly under his arm and he got away into the darkness of the outer world with a laugh and Sofia's one and only prized violin.

Klaus and Sofia returned from their night of escapades into gambling and stepped out of their shirts and pants and into evening gowns and robes. There in the house they delighted in tea and in the fireplace. Rounding the spiral stair, Sofia caught notice of the remnant of a recently burning candlestick, all alone there on the floor at the foot of the staircase. Just as she began investigating, there from the back of the mansion, Klaus was uncovering the show of forced entry that left a back door slightly ajar.

They met each other in the midst of their discovery that they had been the victims of burglary and invasion by an unknown transgressor.

So Sofia made a thorough inspection of her house, hoping to find no displacement of property. Unfortunately she made a regretful discovery. The unguarded spot which sheltered her Stradivarius now stood vacant and bereft of its box.

She told this to Klaus who clenched one fist while smoothing hair back from his forehead and snickering a wry laugh in mockery of how clever this thief thought he had been. Sofia stood determined to report the crime to police and summon an inquiry, but then Klaus was on the other side of the law. So he said with assurance and an air of distant reproach that he would handle the business himself.

30

Klaus had his dogs and his thugs and every available man on every corner and trap house. He went to a hideout of a known felon and he worked his hand and his reputation and he played it real cool. During their exchanges, he overheard who was snitching in the hood. After returning to the mansion, he told Sofia he would be away and that they had been played like fools but that he had the goods on a thief and a very sorry man. So he took some cash and went looking.

Klaus went down to the flats there by way of the steel mills down by the village looking for a man named Chatty, who kicked it in the low parts of town. When he got to the strip, he walked the walkway and met a strange woman and asked her for some company. She asked him if he was the police and he said no. She brought out a condom and they sat in his car and as she performed on him he began muttering about Chatty. When she had finished him off she threw away the junk. She put on some lip stick and Klaus handed her some cash and said he was looking to score a gold chain and a diamond earing. "What about Chatty, do you know him?" and she said "Sure, I know him." Then she looked at the cash and asked "Is that all?"

He slipped her a few more, and she said "Yeah, he's at Defranco's."

Klaus asked where to take her and she said "Down the street to the next block," and when he had dropped her off, he made his way to see Defranco about a snitch they both knew.

After a few minutes work and a few hundred in cash, the man called Chatty gave up the name of the thief and his girl, who lived in the low end, and who had come across a musical instrument, such as a violin or a cello, or something like that. Then he snatched up the money and ran off with his black eyes and his bloody nose.

31

Down in the low end, the thief's heartless mind was set on the ruin of the image of Sofia.

"They'll never suspect us," bragged the thief.

"Did you get it?" asked his girl.

"I've got better than that," stated the thief.

"Do you have it then?" she gibed impatiently. His girl was impetuous sometimes to the point of being subversive to her own misdeeds.

"The bitch had it coming," said the thief.

"Show me then." demanded his girl.

They had never taken him for a thief as he sat at the bar that night. He revealed the precious instrument from within its lusty chamber and out into the dull tableside lamplight, burning with the gas of inexhaustible envy and malapropisms.

He blurted out of turn,

"We'll burn it and smash it to pieces." cried the thief.

"No! It will lead us to the money, you stupid. The price of it alone would take us out of this dump and into the high end."

It was a shadowy heartless ransom for two entwined in a robbery and the separation of Sofia from her object of exploitation.

The thief held the violin high above his head where his girl could not reach.

"There is more to this now. I want what's coming to me."

"Why you horny bastard!" exclaimed the woman and laughed.

They hid it and they covered it and they tucked it away for the time when their efforts would come to light with a bidder and an easer of sorts; someone who would deal in stolen goods and the thief knew right where to go.

32

Sometime soon thereafter, the thief sought the perverse understanding of Sydney the vendor and trafficker. He brought the violin in concealment to a place on the waterfront near where the marina and the breakwall made safe harbor, and he boarded Sydney's boat to make a deal.

The thief inquired about Sydney and a well-dressed brown-skinned coolie led him deep inside the boat to Sydney's lair.

The thief sniffled.

"I have a piece and I want cash for it."

"Got what?" Sydney replied, "And how do you know me?"

"Your name gets thrown around where I'm from."

"I don't know where you're from, but where I'm from we don't do business dressed like that." Sydney chided in derision.

"I'm down on my luck." grumbled the thief.

"I would guess more than that. You're a junkie," snarled Sydney, thinking he should kidnap and sell the man.

"So are you gonna make me an offer or what?"

"I don't know if I'm into that just yet."

"You haven't seen it." said the thief with pride.

"So bring it here."

The thief lay the box and the instrument in front of the man Sydney, the investor and the connoisseur, who said,

"Where'd you happen to come by this?"

"At the mansion. The one at Bellemonte Strada."

Sydney recognized the name, and he knew it was millionaire's row, so he thought, and he capitalized on the thief's mendacity, and said,

"I'll give you a thousand," knowing it would bring him a lot more.

And the thief said that was good enough for his girl, so he took it.

Later, while the thief was busy arguing with his woman on the phone, Klaus came knocking on his door. When it was opened, Klaus made it abundantly clear that a reckoning and an awakening would be happening very soon. So he asked the thief who had it, saying he wanted to buy it, and the thief said that for a fee he'd tell him where it was. Klaus kept up appearances and gave the thief more cash and the thief laid out that it was in the hands of a man named Sydney and then told him where he laid anchor.

So as soon as Klaus heard this he wanted his money's worth of revenge.

At that, Klaus threw the thief down the stairs and he slowly followed him down to the floor while the thief still struggled to rise to his feet after having had his brains throttled.

"I can help you with that." said Klaus, and he kicked him in the head and the face saying,

"Don't bother getting up."

He hit him again in the face breaking his nose and knocking out his front teeth.

33

When Klaus had found the boat moored at anchor at the waterfront near the wharf, he hardened himself and got up his nerve. He found Sydney inside, and then he recognized the grotesque man endowed with great corpulence and surrounded by a group of well dressed, well groomed coolies in fine watches, laid back in comfort and preparedness. Klaus knew that Sydney had a black heart and a pit for a soul because he had run with him in the streets.

He sat among the coolies who eyed him with perspicuity of his near plight, unknown to him as yet, while the pitch and the sway of the yacht on the windy day exacerbated nerves and spun him around in his head.

Sydney sat idly, lazily on his armchair, drumming his fingers on the rest, amused, and took notice of Klaus in his black leather and remained stolid and ambivalent, yet very amorphous like an amoeba. Then Klaus spoke in a slow falsetto voice without any admission that he knew who Sydney was. He said, matter of factly,

"The gig is up. You have what's mine, and I want it back."

Sydney's eyes lit up when he heard the man's voice, and he began massaging the butt end of his chair, caressing the smoothness of the luster and the shine. Recognizing that voice, he was thrown back into the street and what had been done to him in the past, back to the drug trade and the theft of persons, and of human trafficking where he was forced to compete to survive.

He remembered that this man in front of him had played a role, and had stood in the way of his business. So now, wanting to settle the score, Sydney said to the man,

"You don't know what you're asking for. You're playing a dangerous game once again, and I think you know what I mean. I know I had not recognized you but I recognize that voice. You and I have history together. We come from the same parts and we go back don't we? So here's what I'm going to tell you- go home and pack. Take some time off. If you're still around in twenty four hours, I'm coming after you, and I'm gonna send you down the road. And from that you won't ever come back."

Having been uncovered, Klaus became very still and very uneasy. Unable to leave well enough alone, knowing it meant so much to Sofia, he sneered at the fat man, saying,

"We're not finished with this just yet."

When he got up he looked defeated and made a lunge for the dark and grotesque man, threatening him, and at once the coolies, who were on hand to do a duty to Sydney, overpowered Klaus and took him from the quarters and onto the deck and down the walkway and left him salty on the pier, at the wharf, in the wind. He took a last look at the yacht, which he might never see again, and he went back to Sofia, to plan his next move.

Klaus brooded vengefully. *Fiends will stop at nothing to be high again,* he thought, and Sydney was no exception. He should take Sofia and be gone. Leave it lost and forgotten. No. He should pry it from that man's undignified hands and defy his threats and call riot to his door with some of his underground hoods and delinquents. Yes. That is what will manifest on Sydney for his guilt in Sofia's loss of her violin.

34

After Klaus had been removed, Sydney contemplated the attachment that Klaus had to the artifact in his possession and its now inanimate spirit by his own hand. He pried the implement from its box ever so gently with his pudgy fingers and began to examine its reliefs and its curvaceousness, its torsion, and its nuptials at the neck. He admired its dominant hue of burnt umber seduced with red and stressed with black frets, and he extrapolated its value in carnal terms and in human cost, because whoever wanted this back would surely have something valuable to give, namely their life.

He set aside the piece and extricated paper and pen from the hiding place, and he fabricated his legal interest in said artifact and of its provenance which he inquired from the keepers of records. He put out the request and the coolies took it and their replies back and forth, until Sydney became the recipient of good and terrible news.

He slit open the envelope from the keeper with a pointed sharpened edge, and he laid out the crease and he read, with sinister glee, that his artifact was a four hundred year old Stradivarius belonging to Johann Sebastian Bach and now in the hands of its current rightful owner Sofia Amadia, the one time world re-nown eximious performer of strings.

He felt alarmed, and amused, and diabolical all at once. He would have her around his finger with his hand in her pocket in no time at all, with nothing warranting. So he returned to his écrivain and he rolled back the top and into the inky well he dove, and he sang a song sweetly and with maligned exigencies, tempting Sofia with world travel, as if she had nothing and had never been removed and never been kept, and he sealed it with a ribbon and a kiss. He addressed it the eminent Sofia, and off with a coolie it went.

35

Sydney's man carried the letter expeditiously to the waiting Sofia, and in the brightness of day, an unflappable Sofia read the solicitous serenade of Sydney, scriven in his beautiful calligraphy, blackmailing her with her damnable past, and her profligate way of life at Albrecht's expense. Sydney force fed her her own shit. She continued to read as Sydney outlined in great detail what would come next. He was bent on harvesting her body and its service to him on his yacht in a limelight of underground exploits, notably criminal, and if she weren't to comply he would ruin her not only for her tarnished image and her sins, but for her love of Klaus, the felon playboy. Klaus would die or he would be ripped away from her forever, whatever her choice, if she delayed his request. So she wept for the loss of her only expressions: her music and her lover. It was indeed a dark cruel world and she had been dragged down into its laws of petty backstabbing and exploitation and enslavement. She rallied with a thought of retribution in the end. After all this would come redemption.

The world suddenly went black. She had been a cold hardened woman until she entrapped Klaus. He had weakened her, but now she felt she mistreated him. Everything was spiraling around her, as though she had been left cursed on the HMS Burgundian and sent adrift to be captured by the nymph Calypso. There would be no more connections with her son, and Klaus would need her commitments to Sydney in order to survive, alone without her, and she didn't have the strength to resist. Her lip quivered in bitterness and rage and spite for this vermin known as Sydney.

With a sense of self sacrifice, Sofia took paper and pen and wrote,

"My dearest Klaus,

I have gone away. Do not look for me, you will not find me.

Do not waste time. Take what you want from here, leave behind what you don't.

You haven't much time. Though we may never see each other again, it is better that we each live.

Farewell my love,

Sofia"

She resigned herself to subservience to Sydney, and she disposed of the hateful bit of parchment. She packed a bag, and scrubbed away her makeup. Then she lit the lamp for Klaus and she left her mansion with her bank drafts unfilled, and with false promises. She would need to search deep inside herself for past instinct.

Thus, without warning, she fled her gracious life and directed her driver to take her in her black turbo to the waterfront without questions and without happiness.

36

When Klaus returned from Sydney's yacht, he saw that the lights were on. When he entered the mansion expecting to see Sofia and she was nowhere to be found, in any room, in any hallway or anywhere else, he tensed. He had opened locked doors and searched his mind for the right motivation and had found it. He would overtake Sydney with or without Sofia's approval, but even then he wanted to explain himself and his plans for capturing her instrument without alerting her to Sydney's ultimatum for him to be gone.

Her Benz was in its garage and the driver was looking bewildered as he stared up at Klaus sadly. Having not found Sofia at home, Klaus questioned him.

"To where did you take Sofia?" asked Klaus.

"She is gone, my friend." the driver replied.

"To where?"

"Away, she says. Not to be coming back."

"What do you mean away? And what do you mean not to come back?"

"I left her at the waterfront, and she instructed me to drive back here."

Klaus stomped back into the mansion. He entered the large front room and flooded it with light. Then, when he turned, he found there on the mantle, a letter. It was from Sofia, and after he read it, it fell from his hand, onto the marble floor, and he prepared to take the fight to Sydney.

But Sydney wasted no time. The moment that Sofia set foot on the yacht he directed the coolies to call in that old debt of Klaus, and as he prepared in the mansion, a bevy of thugs accompanied by the coolies, penetrated his sanctuary and rolled up on him in the nascence of his plots of revenge, and they exercised the long reach of Sydney. They tied him up with rope and gagged and hooded him. They stole his fine, expensive gold chain, and his rings, and they dragged him out the front of his mansion by his feet, and his head bounced on the pavement. They threw him like a duffel into the back of a waiting car, and took him to the port where they sold him as a slave to an outgoing frigate, bound for Buenos Aires.

37

Sydney did all of the things and exhibited all of the mannerisms of a chauvinistic abuser.

During the long voyages from harbor to port to cities along the Mediterranean, he was dutiful to his dealing and smuggling, keeping Sofia locked in the yacht, only to be removed and placed naked on a stage for indulgent hands and eyes, not so unfamiliar to her and her past fortitude. She did this for Sydney and his thwart and rift of law and order.

From Sicily to Croatia and Lebanon to Egypt, he used her credit, and with her bank accounts he satisfied his passion for human cargo, wholesaling and retailing refugees from the comfort of his yacht while *they* were loaded onto speedy inboards and propelled from Africa and Syria to the highest bidder in the network of slavers; those who crept through the inner cities of the north and south. Those who fed their masochism, their lust, their addictions, and their indolence with the work and the sweat and the weariness in the body and in the mind of a cull of worthless migrant.

A meeting of prospective buyers who had gathered aboard the yacht were looking at Sofia as wolves who stare down prey. They were there to discuss a deal with Sydney but for the advantages of haggling out a bargain, they had put him in a position of having to come from behind to make it work. Believing that they were not accustomed to good hospitality, Sydney thought he would sweeten the deal. He looked to Sofia.

"C'm'ere babe." sang Sydney. "I want you to meet some friends of mine."

Playing it off as though he wouldn't be sharing his only prized possession, he said,

"I'm in a good mood today, why don't you shake some ass. Put on that old show that you used to do, remember the one I mean ? The one you left Albrecht for?" Trying to guilt her again.

He seized her around the waist with his giant arm and he drew her in close and she was reminded of some John, as she resurrected her former self. Though she broadcasted willingness, she was disgusted. Sydney said to the other men in the room,

"For the pleasure of her company, I want two-fifty a head and no less."

But Sofia had a plan.

38

Anchored off shore, the bulk of Sydney's yacht rocked back and forth with meditative ceaselessness to the point of drudgery, boredom and ennui. Sydney was ashore in the business of smuggling again. He had left her on the boat to ensure she could not escape. She roamed the cabin and she stared at the violin box in disgust, similar to the time when she had left it and her music behind for the benefit of her son. She changed into a gray bikini, and she wandered out fruitlessly and unprofitably onto the deck, she was sure. She stared out into the horizon, into nothingness. Sofia thought of Klaus. She fretted about her future and what end this would have to come to. She gripped the rail with an overhand grip and an underhand embrace and she contemplated her experiences and her willingness to throw herself overboard. She felt the muscles tightening in her abdomen, as she was fraught with indecision. The deceit with which she made a portrayal of herself and her devotion to Sydney was a fantasy she played into.

Her money was disappearing into Sydney's black market and she was without Klaus or Albrecht or their son. But she would stay true to her plans.

She loitered at the rail as the day ushered in clouds. She retreated in her mind to *Der Sturm*, and to Beethoven in C minor. And she thought of the fate of the HMS Burgundian. She could not throw herself overboard. So she removed herself from Sydney while the waves all around her reared up in tyranny, and as the winds collided with the stillness, they chilled and tempered her already cold soul.

Sydney, the overgrown wicked cupid, returned from his duties to a shipment of migrants. And she let him touch her skin again.

He grabbed her by the wrist and he led her to the cabin, to the écrivain and he jammed a pen into her hand while he hovered over her and a bank draft for many thousands of dollars of her money. He forced her to sign it away to him and the blackness of his heart at great depth.

39

Stealthily and inconspicuously idling the calm seas off of the coast of Crimea, Sydney prepared for his next venture with Varlomei, the oligarch, consular, and billionaire swindler, and weighed the likelihood of easing into a slave route through the Black Sea to Russia. His want was to insert more stolen and disparaging flesh into the markets that were presided over by Varlomei with his threats and his bribery and with his militants and agents with border control.

Sydney groomed himself lovingly. His pants and shirt had been laid out with their creases and their starch. He tucked in his shirt and fastened his suspenders as he buttoned his vestments. He slid on his oversized gold and ruby ring and he clasped the back of his vintage swiss chronometer behind his wrist and rotated the bezel clockwise and in sync with the changing time. He took a walk around the cabin noticing, and setting up his props, then went to find Sofia to command her to adorn herself in a minimalist way, and that she should remain loose so that no formalities would stand in the way of what would come next. The violin would stay hidden away so as not to tempt Varlomei into tilting the playing field. The boat that carried Varlomei appeared in the distance, answering the turns of the coastline, and was fast approaching. Sofia sat on the mid level with a coolie, while Sydney and the others waited within the dim light of the deck, hopeful and impatient. While the coolie looked away, Sofia filled her palm with sedatives, and swallowed them with a chianti brought with them from Milan. She took more than for a teaser and less than for oblivion. Sydney would not want her incoherent.

The ship got even with the prow of Sydney's yacht and a rope bridge was thrown aboard, and Varlomei's retinue spearheaded the precess of Varlomei and his own preeminent grounds. He crossed over the last rung and met Sydney with a cigarette in one hand and a handshake in the other.

They descended to the mid level of the boat where Sofia was lax and on hand, while Varlomei sat and Sydney lowered into his arm chair with the mahogany rests. Through Sofia's haze she heard them as they spoke in a foreign language. They spoke slowly and they caressed their words. They began drinking Rakia that Sydney had set aside for the negotiation. They got drunk and put off an impending agreement for the moment, because they were enjoying themselves but more importantly because Sydney had a card up his sleeve. So when they were liquored, they sang impassionately together in a sad, slow farewell to Slavianka and her trials in a Russian patriotic song, and there was romp and carousing that continued until Varlomei set down his glass. That was a signal to Sydney. He had been warming up for the coup de grâce. He licked his lips and massaged his forearm and he got up off of the armchair as he looked to Sofia and beckoned her to come to him. She doggedly led her attention to the bedroom off of the cabin and undressed. Sydney said something to Varlomei in Turkish and Varlomei smiled with entitlement. He crossed slowly over to the bedroom, and there Sofia lay naked, and he admired her aging skin, her tan lines, her shaved pussy and her small tits. Without haste, he exposed his white, hairless chest and pulled out an uncut dick and he pushed her to the side, and she, in her haze, rolled to her flank and put up her leg. He went in the back way, saying something in English trying to sound sexy, then cursed the refugees, until he came and she grunted. He used her clothes to wipe himself off, and he got up to dress when she rolled onto her back to face him with much in mind, too much for Varlomei. He found the look similar to victory and he smiled and said to her to be a good little Katyusha, and she looked away with a breath and with something reserved for someone else.

Varlomei reentered the cabin where Sydney was massaging his mahogany armrests and said to Varlomei,

"We are more than friends now, Varlomei, aren't we? And friends help each other out, don't they? My people need your people and you need my toil in your sweatshops, so here's what I'm proposing - I get two hundred and fifty a head for the first thousand, and that will make it effortless to you. We'll talk specifics later for another thousand or more."

"Fine, Sydney, I will send you the money and you send me the Somalian refuse."

The coolies escorted Varlomei and his entourage from the upper levels out onto the gangplank, and he staggered back to his yacht. The boat slid away and only the darkness remained.

Sydney entered the spare room off of the cabin and retrieved the violin. He gloated over it and returned to find Sofia at the couch dressed again. So he told her to play something in triumph but she scoffed at him. He slapped her in the face with a free hand and it stung her cheek and rung her addled brain. She fumbled with the box and she sidled in and out of hollows and spikes of awareness, grabbing the violin with too much haste, and almost fell. She righted herself and finding her chin barely, she exercised the bow and crossed the strings with unanimated disharmony. Sydney laughed menacingly, obviously disapproving of her apathetic approach to his merriment. She went into a piece by Kachaturian, while Sydney watched her for a short time until his head slowly fell into his chest and he went to sleep.

Sofia hid the violin in her bedroom and replaced the empty locked box in the spare room, without the key. She was then so relaxed and on the verge of somniferous ecstasy that she collapsed onto her bed.

Following the night with Vladimir Sofia disavowed herself of Sydney's uses for her, and in a rage, she blurted out,

"I'm mad, I'm sad and I hate you."

She slammed the door, and stormed into the bathroom. She flushed away her bloody rag and for whatever her reasons were, she cursed his ego, his mistreatment, and his thoughtlessness. She cursed also her own plans.

40

That night as she lay in her bed, she dreamt. She had visions. She looked out from the end of a great hallway, and saw a flood, like a river of blue water flowing violently through it, reaching both sides of it, and it was coming toward her in white foam and with speed and it was washing away wooden chairs and mahogany tables and strange helpless people. And in the flow, she saw Albrecht, and beyond him Marie, and they were drowning. And then the water reached her and she was buoyed up into it. But then she saw Sydney and he was above it all, and he was extending his hand to her, from a life raft or from the shore, and she was about to take it, but she was calm and peaceful in the water, and it was warm. Then suddenly she was in motion, and swept into a room with the water and the door was shut, keeping her in, and the room is filled with knee deep water, and after looking, she could not find the key to open the door so she tried the knob and it opened. She went out onto the deck of the yacht, from the door, and she dove head first out into the water, the blue water, without fear or hesitation. In her hand was her violin, her right hand, and as she fell deeper, she let it go and it descended down to the bottom, and then she hung motionless in the water.

41

Sydney brought Sofia as his trophy one summer afternoon when the storms had kept him at the waterfront, and at the dock, and he led her to the underground again. There was a gathering of pashas, and gamblers and men looking to procure whatever they could profit from, so she made herself enviable, as it was part of her plan.

She fluttered and swirled the paper folds of a colorful sensu, an oriental bamboo fan, round about her face, in a partially secret and partially candid gesture. With it, she maintained one captive audience, a man named Roen, whose game was black market art. He was known to supplement his speculation with the fetishes of women. He acted coy, but she was determined, so she threw her charms all around him. She had never stopped playing the part of the self-assured predator, a part that drove her.

And though Sydney kept her close, and he overindulged in the glow of other men's attention, he remained wary and skeptical and was careful not to be taken in by any of the pashas, and she was careful not to be lured away from Sydney because she didn't want to be a medium of exchange. She needed to be out of Sydney's grasp and in possession of the man across the table who admired her for her own interest, and its price and its caveat unknown to him. So she extended an invitation to the man while Sydney was preoccupied with the camaraderie, expressing her need to be alone with him aboard the yacht, with a sidelong glance toward Sydney and up away toward the harbor. She reminded Sydney of the where and the when he must release her, so that she may return to her room to sleep. She suggested that the art dealer should bind her to her promise to remain aboard the yacht and wait for his return. Sydney was drunk and so he commanded a coolie and the man named Roen to take Sofia to the boat and use her if he promised to cut him in on any deal.

They left from the room and the three of them then took the man's car straight to the waterfront and to the empty yacht. In the dark on the deck, Roen gave the coolie a Turkish cigar and told him he needed a minute alone, where and when Sofia took Roen into the recesses of the boat. She led him to the bedroom with turbulence and she uncovered the Stradivarius, declaring insincerely and wholeheartedly that it belonged to Sydney and she wanted it to go away because it reminded him of someone else and not her. So Roen looked at it and he studied it while Sofia held a light close. He saw how genuine and how pristine it was, and he said,

"If I'm to pay you for this, what about Sydney?"

"He doesn't want my freedom so it shouldn't matter to us."

Roen thought and he concluded that Sydney wasn't a real issue anyway, so he replied,

"Take what I offer you and I will return with the money in one month's time."

And she said, "Very well."

Roen left the yacht and thus ended act one to the plan of Sofia. She was amazed at her own cunning, and the thought benefited her sense of self and of relief.

42

A month later, after he lured Sydney back to Istanbul with a tale of an underground jaipur who wanted to make a trade in black market goods, Roen, the buyer, the art profiteer, returned. He came with details pertaining to an account in her name. Sydney had been let loose on the world once again, and after he had left Sofia to herself without coolies and anchored offshore, she prepared to perform her second act in a life-sized diarama of emancipation and its bounty for her and her piece. So Roen snuck into Sydney's lair unmolested, and he brought with him her payout. From the deck to the door, as his eyes glittered with triumph, he gladly swore that her benefit was to be in the millions. She was only so happy and collected the Stradivarius from her bedroom, and gave it to him, and he cradled it in his hands and said,

"That's that, so I will leave you now."

He held it close and he prepared to leave when she reached for him with an arm that she threw around his neck and she cooed.

"That isn't the way I want this to end."

He was keen on her again and in retrospect it was because of her unavailability, but he said,

"What do you mean by that?"

She undid a button of his shirt and put a hand to his chest and stroked his chest hair, as he succumbed to the weight of too much unexpected happiness all at once, and said,

"I don't know what you see in Sydney."

She looked away quickly then up into his eyes as though she needed to find something to say because she knew she was good at what she was doing, and wanted not to appear so. But he didn't catch on, and he had everything to gain. Before he could tell her how it was going to be, she said,

"Take me with you," even though she knew that there was danger involving him with Sydney.

But Roen remained a staunch defender of her honor, and his own love for risk, adventure, and romance, so he said to her,

"You have ten minutes. Pack your things. We're going away to Crete where we can stay famously free."

Sofia left at that moment with only the clothes on her back, and turning to look at the yacht while they descended to Roen's speedboat, she was hopeful that Sydney would not catch up with them. Once in the boat, Roen gripped the throttle tightly and pressed forward, and the speedboat roared with a sound like a rampant lion. They faced nothing but open sea between them and wherever they were going, she didn't care. Roen said that he would take them on an indirect route to Crete, as he had said before, by way of the islands of the Dodecanese, then to Santerini and finally Iraklio where they would be welcomed as Greeks from Samos with his passport and she as a visiting performer.

43

The port city of Iraklio was always in mourning over the death of any new way of life, always hanging on to tradition as they did. There, they docked and entered the city looking for a dwelling among the plaster and stone traditionalism. He rented a place as she, without angst, pushed the thought of her money out of her mind and went to sleep.

When she woke, she saw that Roen had filled the room with flagons of muscat and bowls of large, brown kalamata olives in vinegar and olive oil, so she sat at a table across from him and wondered what her next move should be.

"I thought we could eat and enjoy Crete," he said. "I know you want to keep your Stradivarius."

She thought about it a minute.

"What about you and I?" she asked.

"I have other art sales I make here in Crete. I thought you would like to stay here with me."

So she kept her violin and she played for him, while he worked there in Crete, and they were happy and they remained there indefinitely as an old flame flickered and died and a new partnership began.

The End

Milton Keynes UK
Ingram Content Group UK Ltd.
UKHW020204241123
433069UK00007B/227/J

9 798822 928282